Soggy Moggie:
A Christmas Cat Tale

Devised and Written by Jason Smith

Illustrated by Hayley Kershaw

Soggy Moggie: A Christmas Cat Tale

Message from the author

Thank you for buying our Christmas book. While our first book 'A New Hero' was very much a short cat tale introducing Soggy Moggie to the world, our Christmas book is a much longer and rather bushier cat tale.

The story is an amalgamation of a few short stories that I received in my dreams, each one has an important message to share with the reader and I think all are woven in to a fun tapestry of an exciting cat adventure.

Each new character brings with them a unique back-story and personality which I think makes the book engaging for the reader. Again, I would like to thank the wonderful artist Hayley Kershaw for bringing the characters to life.

Enjoy the Christmas adventures of Soggy Moggie and his friends and remember bravery comes from the heart and not an object.

Dedication

I would like to dedicate this book to my late cat of 16 years, a true and dear friend, the beautiful fluff ball Truffle.

Want to read more about Soggy Moggie and his friends?

Visit our website with character profiles and games at www.soggymoggie.uk or scan the QR code on the back of the book with your smart phone to find out more about the Soggy Moggie universe.

Who is Soggy Moggie?

Moggie Smith was named Soggy Moggie because he is not afraid of water.

Moggie wears his medal for bravery and can use the power of water to help others.

Moggie is the bravest cat on the block and he is a hero to all the cats in the alleys.

Moggie and his friends are always there to help animals in need.

Meet Soggy Moggie's friends.

Kittykins

Kittykins is Moggie's best friend.

Kittykins is very kind and likes sharing.

Kittykins lives at the Kind Spa health resort.

Moggie saved Kittykins from being bullied.

'Spooky' Si

Si is called Spooky because he can do magic.

Si uses his magic to help good cats.

Si lives in a cave in the woods.

Moggie saved Si from the Shadow Cats.

Teddy

Teddy and Moggie are good friends.

Teddy is a small kitten but is brave.

Teddy lives in the alley with his family.

Moggie saved Teddy from drowning.

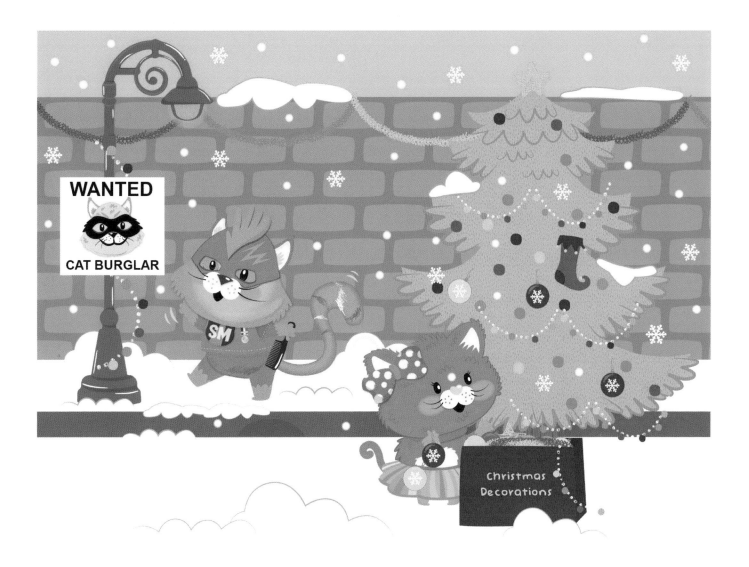

It is two weeks until Christmas Day. Moggie is helping Kittykins trim up the alleys.

Kittykins has put tinsel on the alley walls and is decorating the Christmas tree.

I'm so excited; I can't wait for Christmas", says Kittykins; "I hope Papa Paws visits", she added.

Moggie is reading a wanted poster on the alley lamppost for a thief called Cat Burglar.

Putting up decorations is hard work so Kittykins goes to the shop for some snacks.

Kittykins buys salmon flavour milkshakes for her and Moggie from Feline Foods.

As Kittykins walks out of the shop she sees a robbery taking place at toy shop Catibobs.

It's Cat Burglar, the cat that is wanted for robbery; he is carrying a stolen mouse car toy.

Kittykins shouts to Cat Burglar to give the toys back to the shop.

"Catch me if you can!" says Burglar as he runs down the street.

Kittykins chases Burglar but her legs are too small and she cannot catch him.

Cat Burglar is very fast and jumps over a trash can as he runs towards the alley.

Moggie corners Cat Burglar in the alley and says "I am Soggy Moggie and I am a hero!"

"Give the toys back", says Moggie. Cat Burglar refuses and says "Catch me if you can!"

To prove his bravery Moggie pours water over his head and combs back his wet hair.

Cat Burglar is shocked as he can't believe a cat is not afraid of water.

"You might be brave but nobody can catch the Cat Burglar", said Burglar.

Moggie drinks some water and squirts it at Burglar.

Burglar laughs and cartwheels to avoid the water and runs down the alley.

Moggie tries to chase Burglar but the Burglar is too fast and escapes.

Moggie goes in search of Cat Burglar, looking for clues of where he is hiding.

Moggie meets a group of birds who are singing Christmas carols and stops to listen.

Moggie hears a scream in the distance and climbs up a tree to see what is happening.

In the distance Moggie sees a tall castle and Cat Burglar climbing in through the window.

Cat Burglar jumps in through the window of the large castle.

The room is full of expensive furniture, jewels and gold.

A female cat is in the room and is shouting for help screaming "Stop this thief!".

Cat Burglar ignores the cat and he starts putting all the jewels and gold into his sack.

Moggie jumps in the window and confronts the Cat Burglar.

"I am here to save the day", says Moggie, "Drop those jewels!" he added.

"Catch me if you can!" says Cat Burglar as he puts the sack over his shoulder.

Moggie pulls out a bottle of water and pours some over his head and combs his hair.

Moggie drinks some water and squirts it towards Cat Burglar.

Cat Burglar somersaults over Moggie avoiding the water but drops the sack of jewels.

Moggie turns around but Burglar has already jumped out of the window and escaped.

Cat Burglar jumps onto a tree and uses his tail to swing away on the trees.

"Thank you for saving my jewels", said the cat. "That's ok, I am a hero", said Moggie.

"My name is Princess Truffle, I am very rich and very important", she said.

"How much shall I pay you for saving my jewels?" said Princess Truffle.

"Heroes don't work for money, we are heroes because we like to help", said Moggie.

"You are a hero and you are very brave", said Princess Truffle.

"Oh no! I think the burglar has stolen my medal for bravery", said Moggie.

"Don't worry, just buy a new one", said Princess Truffle.

"You can't buy bravery", said Moggie as he waved goodbye to the Princess.

Moggie is walking back from the castle and sees a kitten being hunted by a hound dog.

The dog tries to catch the kitten in a net but he trips over and the kitten escapes.

Moggie runs to challenge the dog but stops as he remembers he lost his bravery.

The dog looks at Moggie and barks "another scaredy cat" before walking away.

Moggie visits his friend Spooky Si. Spooky Si lives in a cave and is a magic cat.

Moggie tells Si his medal was stolen and he has lost his bravery.

Si looks in to his magic cat bowl and says "Bravery is not an object, bravery is a feeling".

"I don't understand but thank you", says Moggie as he waves goodbye to his friend Si.

Moggie tells Kittykins about his visit to Si's but that he didn't understand his advice.

Kittykins says "Don't worry I believe in you and I love you, you are my best friend".

"With or without a medal you are the bravest cat I know, you are a hero!" she added.

"You are so kind", said Moggie as he hugged Kittykins and started to feel brave again!

Moggie receives a large post delivery from the post cat Jessica.

There were lots of wrapped presents and a card attached.

The card reads 'Moggie, I have given you lots of presents because I want to be your friend'.

Moggie looks at the note and it is signed by Princess Truffle.

Moggie knocks on Truffle's door. Mr Beaver the butler answers and lets Moggie in.

"Have you come to be my friend?" says Princess Truffle.

"I've come to give you the presents back", said Moggie. The Princess looks shocked!

Moggie teaches the Princess "You can't buy friendship" and Moggie waves goodbye.

It was two days before Christmas and the snow was falling in the alleys.

Moggie was having a snowball fight with his young friend Teddy.

Kittykins and her friend Mittens are playing in the snow and making a snow cat.

The kittens hear cat sleigh bells ringing! Who could this be?

Coming down the alley is the 'cat Father Christmas' Papa Paws riding his cat sleigh.

Papa Paws is a big cat with a big fluffy beard; he is wearing a big red coat.

Papa Paws' sleigh is very fast as it is being pulled by four greyhounds on scooters.

Papa Paws' sleigh is full of presents for the local cats at Christmas.

Cat Burglar drops from a lamppost and lands in Papa Paws' sleigh and pushes him out.

Cat Burglar takes the reins and shouts to the greyhounds to ride away.

Moggie runs towards the sleigh to stop Cat Burglar stealing the presents.

Moggie drinks some water and squirts it in front of the sleigh and the snow turns to ice!

The scooters start to slide on the ice and Papa Paws' sleigh crashes in to the alley wall.

The sleigh lands on top of Moggie as Burglar jumps out just before the crash.

Cat Burglar puts all the presents into his sack, climbs the lamppost and swings away.

By the time Moggie frees himself, Cat Burglar has already disappeared into the trees.

Papa Paws looks sad. "I don't have any more money to buy presents", he says.

Teddy tells Santa not to worry, "Soggy Moggie will find the presents" he says.

The Princess arrives in the alley looking for Moggie and talks to Kittykins.

Kittykins explains that Moggie is on a mission to find Cat Burglar and the presents.

Moggie is in search of Cat Burglar and the presents; he sees a present next to a tree.

Moggie looks up at the tree; it is the tallest tree in town, so tall he cannot see the top.

There was a sign at the bottom of the tree which said 'Danger! Do not climb this tree'.

Moggie wasn't afraid and started to climb the tall tree to investigate.

A delivery cart pulled up at the side of Papa Paws; it was Jessica the post cat.

Jessica says she has a special delivery of lots of presents for Papa Paws.

"Who sent the presents?" asked Papa Paws. "We don't know", said Jessica.

Jessica handed an earring to Kittykins she found in the post bag, maybe it was a clue?

Moggie continued to climb the tree; it was very high but Moggie was not afraid.

The tree was so high that Moggie could see for miles but he couldn't see any clues.

Moggie continued his climb and noticed at the top of the tree was a large tree house.

Moggie heard a noise coming from the tree house so he climbed in to investigate.

The tree house was full of presents and sitting in the tree house was Cat Burglar.

Moggie asked Cat Burglar to give back the presents but Cat Burglar refused.

Moggie squirted water at Burglar who somersaulted over but hit the tree house wall.

The tree house began to tip over and all the presents slid out of the tree house.

Burglar told Moggie that he couldn't defeat him because he had his medal for bravery.

Moggie smiled and poured water over his head and combed back his wet hair.

Burglar was shocked! "How can you be brave when you don't have your medal?" he said.

"I have learned that bravery comes from the heart and not a medal", said Moggie.

Moggie asks Cat Burglar, "Why did you steal the Christmas presents?"

Burglar said, "When I was a kitten we couldn't afford presents so I would steal them."

Moggie taught Cat Burglar, "If you do good deeds and are kind you get lots of gifts."

"I am sorry", said Burglar, who handed back Moggie's medal and they shook paws.

It is Christmas Eve back in the alley. The weather is stormy and the wind is swirling.

Moggie tells Kittykins about Cat Burglar and the presents falling out of the tree house.

Kittykins tells Moggie not to worry as lots of presents were delivered to Papa Paws.

Kittykins shows Moggie the earring which might be a clue as to who sent the presents.

Moggie knocks on Truffle's door. Mr Beaver the butler answers and invites Moggie in.

Moggie hands the earring to Truffle and says "I recognised it was yours", and smiled.

"It was kind of you to buy the presents, please join us for Christmas dinner", said Moggie.

"I would love to come for dinner", said Truffle; they hugged and became good friends.

Moggie is walking back to the alley and sees the hunting dog again chasing kittens.

Moggie tells the dog to stop but the dog just laughs and barks "scaredy cat!" at Moggie.

Moggie drinks some water and squirts it in the air; it freezes and makes an ice sword.

Moggie chases the dog away with the ice sword as the kittens cheer "SOGGY MOGGIE!"

It is Christmas morning, the wind stops blowing. Kittykins shouts "it's snowing!"

"That's not snow", said Moggie, "It's raining Christmas presents!" The friends cheered.

It was the presents that fell from the tree house that were blowing in the sky.

The alleys' homeless kittens are excited and run out to catch the presents.

Moggie and friends sit down to enjoy a Christmas meal of turkey and pigeon pie.

There was a knock on the door; it was Papa Paws. "Join us for dinner", said Moggie.

"I hope you managed to deliver all the presents in time?" said Kittykins.

"I would have run out of time but luckily I had a helper, here he is…" said Papa Paws.

In walks Cat Burglar! "Happy Christmas! My real name is Nimble", said Cat Burglar.

"Soggy Moggie taught me that kindness is the biggest gift of all", said Nimble.

"Welcome Nimble, please join us for dinner, there is plenty of lovely food", said Moggie.

"Moggie and friends have saved Christmas", said Papa Paws as all the friends cheered!

Hope you enjoyed my book

Lots of love,

Soggy Moggie

Jason

Turn the page to see all our wonderful characters...

A Christmas Cat Tale

Kittykins
Best friend

Soggy Moggie
Hero

Teddy
Friend

Nimble
Cat Burglar

Truffle
Princess

Spooky Si
Magic cat

Meet the characters

Muffy
Baby kitten

Papa Paws
Father Christmas

Mr Beaver
Butler

Jessica
Post cat

Rein dogs
Sleigh dogs

Hounder
Hunting dog

Printed in Great Britain
by Amazon

19313122R00025